PAW PATROL™: PUPS SAVE MONKEY-DINGER
A CENTUM BOOK 9781912707430
Published in Great Britain by Centum Books Ltd
First published 2018
This edition published 2021
3 5 7 9 10 8 6 4 2

Centum Books Ltd, 20 Devon Square, Newton Abbot, Devon TQ12 2HR, UK
9/10 Fenian St, Dublin 2, D02 RX24, Ireland
books@centumbooksltd.co.uk
CENTUM BOOKS Limited Reg. No. 07641486

A CIP catalogue record for this book is
available from the British Library

Printed in Great Britain

PUPS SAVE
MONKEY-DINGER

centum

STARRING . . .

TRACKER

SKYE

MAYOR HUMDINGER

CARLOS

CHASE

RYDER

Mayor Humdinger is being grumpy as usual. He's on a holiday tour of the jungle with his Kitten Catastrophe Crew, led by Carlos and Tracker.

"There are too many bugs on this walk and it's too hot!" he complains.

"Don't worry. You'll love the next bit," says Carlos. "We're coming to the Monkey Temple. It's amazing."

"The temple was built thousands of years ago. Be careful," says Tracker.

"I can't see. It's too dark," says the Mayor. "Whaaaaa!" He trips over a tile on the floor and falls on his tummy, triggering a mechanism beneath the stones.

There's a loud rumble and a pillar rises
up with something gold glinting on the top.

"You found the
ancient monkey mask,"
says Tracker. "It's said
to give whoever wears
it the magical power
of a mighty ape."

"Hmm. I like power,"
mutters Mayor Humdinger.

"Ooh, ooh, ooh."

He grabs the mask and puts it on. "Ooh ... I feel strange," he says.

He starts behaving just like a big monkey! Before anyone can stop him he runs for the jungle trees outside. He's going to need rescuing. Time to call the PAW Patrol!

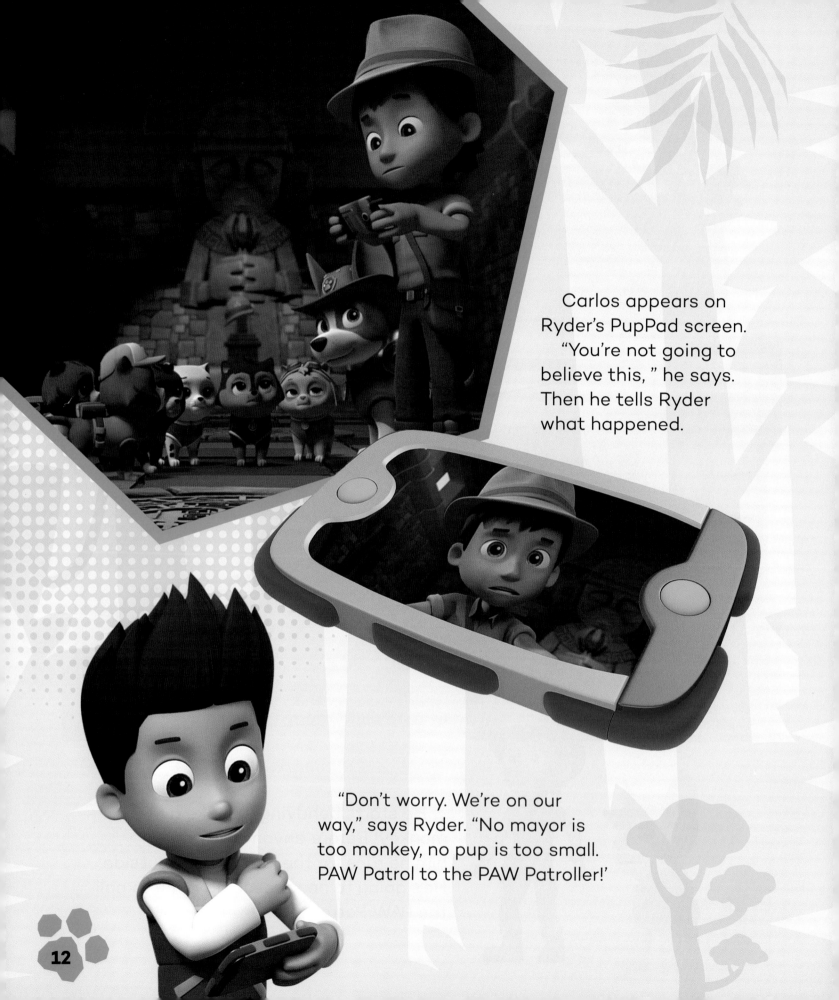

Carlos appears on Ryder's PupPad screen. "You're not going to believe this," he says. Then he tells Ryder what happened.

"Don't worry. We're on our way," says Ryder. "No mayor is too monkey, no pup is too small. PAW Patrol to the PAW Patroller!'

Ryder briefs everyone onboard the PAW Patroller.

"Skye, we need you to use your helicopter and goggles to track Mayor Humdinger from the air. Tracker, we'll need your great hearing to help track him and your cables to rescue him."

"This pup's gotta fly," says Skye.

"I'm all ears!" says Tracker.

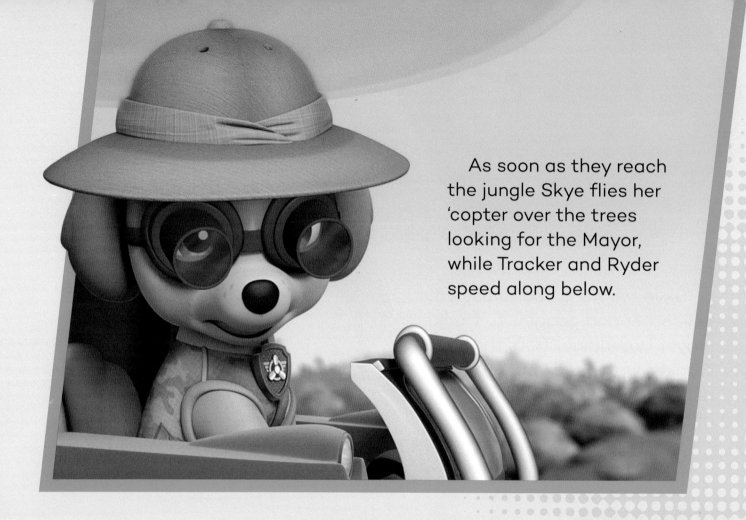

As soon as they reach the jungle Skye flies her 'copter over the trees looking for the Mayor, while Tracker and Ryder speed along below.

"Ruff, ruff. Goggles!" Skye orders. Her goggles zoom in close-up on the ground below but there's no sign of the monkey mayor yet.

Humdinger is busy swinging through the jungle when he meets Mandy the monkey and her family. They think he's lots of fun when he starts juggling coconuts. He's definitely made some new friends!

Tracker hears the monkeys chattering together.

"Ryder, Skye. He's that way," he says pointing towards the noise.

Skye zooms low and spots the Mayor swinging along.

"Follow him," says Ryder. "We're coming as fast as we can."

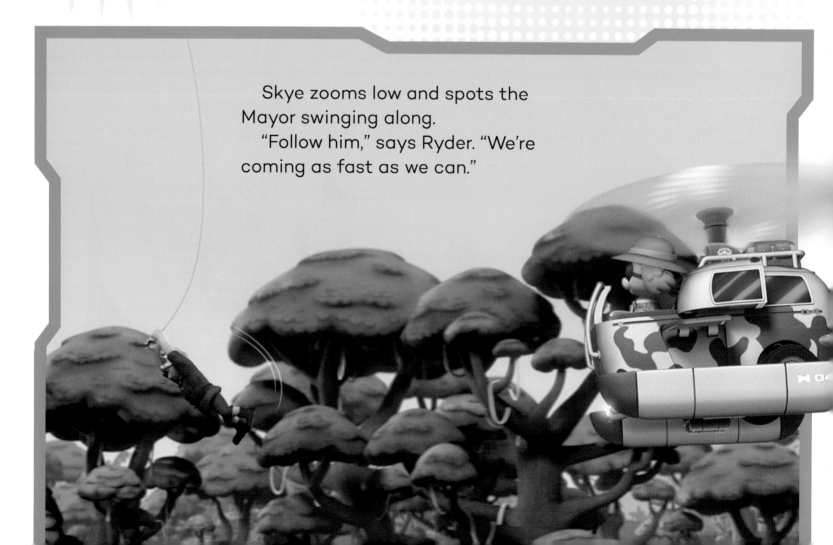

"Ryder, he's heading for a gorge and so are you!" warns Skye.

Ryder and Tracker slam their brakes on just in time, at the very edge of the cliff.

"Well, we found the gorge," says Ryder.

"Phew! It nearly found us!" replies Tracker.

Mayor Humdinger is on the other side of a rope bridge, pulling funny faces and poking out his tongue.

"The bridge isn't safe. There's a loose bridge support," warns Ryder. "Rocky, can you help fix it?"

"Green means go!
I'm on my way,"
calls Rocky.

Soon Rocky is on the scene.
"Ruff. Hammer," he barks and a
hammer extends from his Pup Pack
to knock in the bridge support.

"Let's go," grins Tracker.

"Vamos!"

"Once Ryder reaches the other side, he is ready for action - "Now to find Mayor Humdinger, or should I say Monkeydinger!"

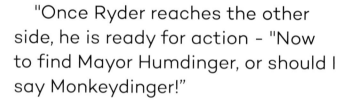

A banana bounces off Ryder's helmet.

"Ruff. Cables," barks Tracker and his cables shoot from his Pup Pack up to the tree.

He swings over for a rescue but the monkey Mayor has other ideas.

He leaps off, spinning Tracker's cables round as he goes.

"I'll distract the Mayor while you grab the mask," says Skye and she hovers her helicopter above the tree.

As the Mayor looks up, Tracker swings by and grabs the mask at last.

Suddenly, the Mayor is himself again. "Help! Where am I? And why do I want to eat bananas so badly?" he cries and clumsily drops out of the tree.

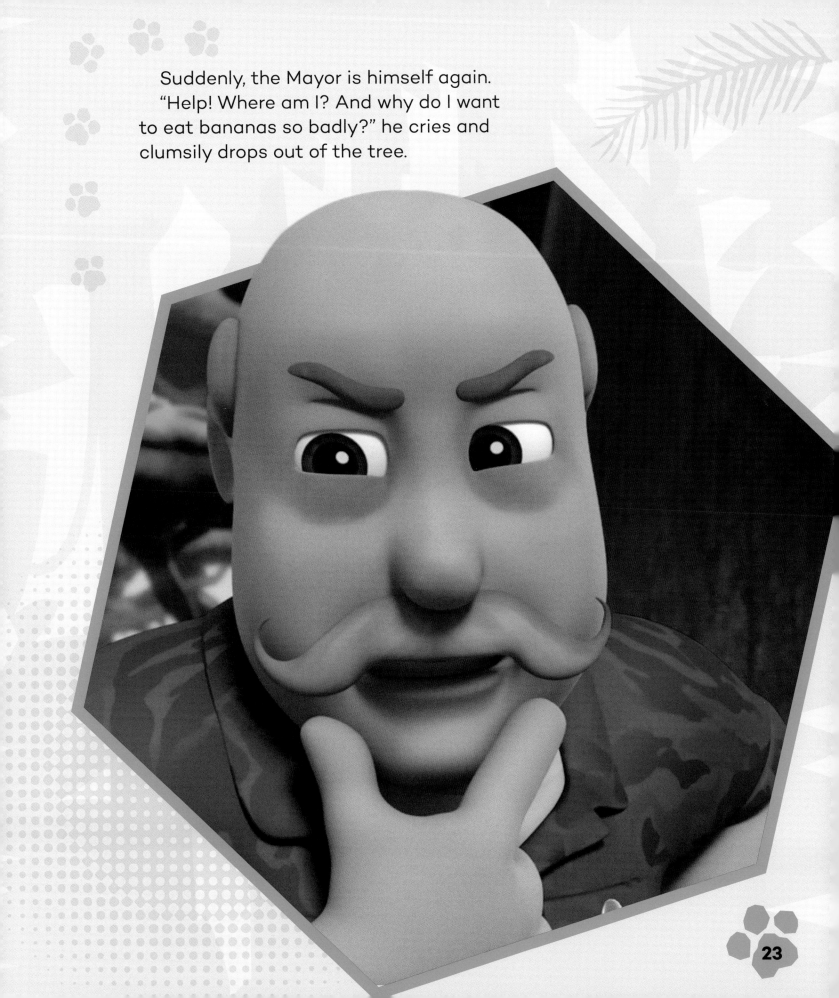

The little monkeys are sad to see their new friend go, so just as he's crossing the rope bridge one of them grabs the mask from Tracker's back.

"No!"

cries Tracker, but the monkey pops the mask back on the Mayor.

"He's going monkey again!" says Ryder as the Mayor leaps onto the very edge of the bridge....

This time the mask falls off for good and the terrified Mayor topples off the bridge towards the gorge below.

"Help!"

he shouts.

He grabs a rope just in time. Now he's dangling in mid-air!

"Skye. Pull the Mayor up with your harness," says Ryder.

The Mayor is far too scared to grab the harness.

"I can't let go of the rope!" he shouts, so Tracker swings over and attaches himself to the harness instead. Then he grabs the Mayor with his grappling hook and finally lifts him to safety.

Soon everyone is back at the Monkey Temple and Mayor Humdinger is looking sheepish.

"Thanks for saving me, Ryder," he says quietly.

"That's okay. Whenever you have a problem just yelp for help," says Ryder.

The golden mask is safe, too. Mandy the monkey has brought it back.

"Keep that thing away from me!" cries Mayor Humdinger. He's still feeling a little monkeyish and he leaps onto a tree branch.
"When did I get so good at climbing?" he asks. "Oh, and by the way. Does anyone have a banana?"

THE END

Are you ruff-ruff ready for a mission? LET'S ROLL!

Mayor Humdinger visits an ancient Monkey Temple with
Carlos and Tracker. He discovers a magical mask and things take a turn
for the worse! Can the PAW Patrol stop the monkey business?

Centum Books Ltd, 20 Devon Square, Newton Abbot,
Devon, TQ12 2HR UK
9/10 Fenian St, Dublin 2, D02 RX24, Ireland
Printed in Great Britain

**Join in every day
on Nick Jr.**
nickjr.co.uk

#631595

ISBN: 978-1-912707-43-0   RRP £5.99
9 781912 707430
TLE02451 - T3.2 - U3 - CEN1038PIC

nickelodeon